HIT THE STREETS

by **Terry Collins**

illustrated by
Artful Doodlers Ltd.

Simon Spotlight/Nickelodeon

New York   London   Toronto   Sydney   Singapore

Based on the TV series *Nickelodeon Rocket Power*® created by Klasky Csupo, Inc. as seen on Nickelodeon®

 SIMON SPOTLIGHT

An imprint of Simon & Schuster Children's Publishing Division
1230 Avenue of the Americas, New York, New York 10020

First Edition   10 9 8 7 6 5 4 3 2 1
ISBN 0-689-85455-2

"Guys! Guys! You gotta see this!" Sam Dullard cried, as he ran into the Shore Shack with his laptop computer held proudly over his head.

"What? You get a high online score for 'Geekiest of the Geeks' again?" Otto Rocket said with a snort. "Big whoop, Sammy."

"Even better than a high score!" Sam replied. "I was doing a search on skateboarding and found a totally rad new extreme sport!"

"Check it out. That dude's lying down on his board," Twister Rodriguez said, looking at the picture on the screen.

"You're supposed to be flat and close to the ground in street luge," Sam said. "You just grab a board and hit the streets!"

"Awesome! I am so totally there," Otto said. "Come on, Twist! We've got another set of wheels to conquer!"

"Wheels to flatten is more like it," Reggie said, snagging Otto by the arm. "In case you haven't noticed, streets have obstacles . . . like cars, trucks, buses."

"So," Otto said. "I don't mind sharing the road."

"Or a hospital bed, little cuz," Tito added. "Your sister is right."

Otto frowned. "Major traffic jam! Maybe Ocean Shores isn't ready for street luge . . . yet!"

"Hey! If we organize a tournament, we can turn everyone on to street luge!" Otto said with a wide smile. "All we gotta do is close down a hilly street and *BAM!*—instant luge course!"

"That's the spirit, Rocket boy," Ray said. "If you guys can find a safe place to practice, the Shore Shack would be willing to cosponsor the tournament."

A few days later the kids arrived at Madtown Skate Park with their new luge boards and safety gear, ready to roll!

Madtown owner, Conroy Blanc, greeted them. Reggie went into her best saleswoman pitch:

"Our dad was hoping you'd cosponsor a street luge tournament, Mr. B," she said. "It's great publicity for both of your businesses!"

"Sounds like a plan! Okay, you have yourself a sponsor," Conroy said with a smile. "I'll make a few phone calls and see about setting up the course on Hightop Lane."

"That would be awesome, Mr. B!" Otto said. "Is it okay if we set up a practice area for street luge here in Madtown?"

"Absolutely," Conroy replied.

The gang quickly learned there was more to street luge than just riding down a hill on a board.

"Keep your arms and legs close to your body and point your feet forward!" Ray called. "You'll be more aerodynamic that way!"

"I don't wanna be more aerodynamic!" Sam yelled.

"Chill, Squid," Twist replied. "Dude, you need to be fierce, 'cause I'm getting it all on film."

"Move, Reg! Otto is on the loose!" Otto said impatiently.

"Like you'd be going this fast if you weren't on my tail," Reggie retorted.

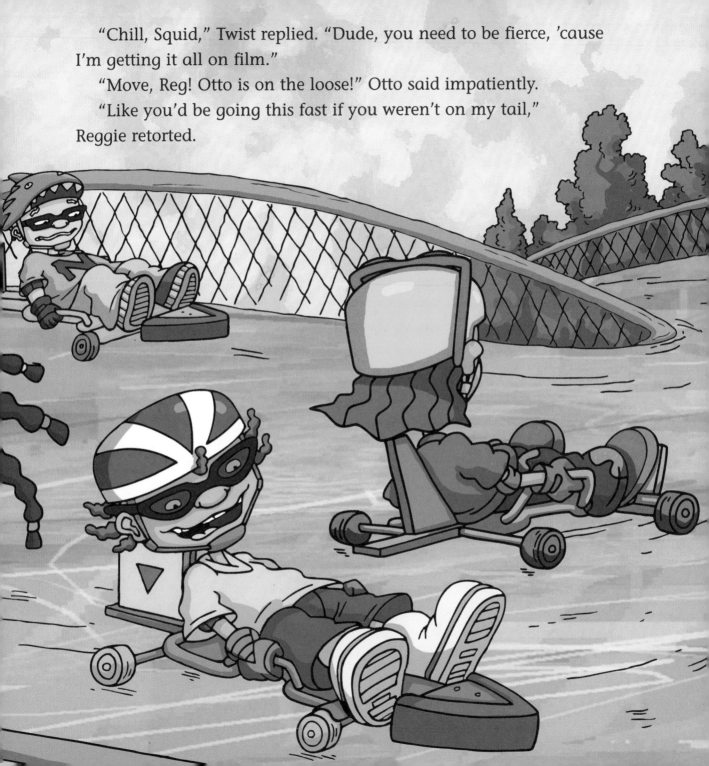

After getting permission from the city to hold the event, the next step was promoting it.

Reggie designed a rad flyer and the gang papered all of Ocean Shores with the time and location of the street luge tournament.

"So far, so good. We've already got twenty people who want to try street luge," Sam said.

"Awesome, Sam," Reggie replied. "I'm so glad you found out about it!"

"Think we'll be ready?" Twister asked as he gave a flyer to some kids.

"Twist, I was born ready," Otto replied confidently.

"I didn't think Saturday was ever going to get here," Otto said, placing the final cone on the tournament course.

Twister yawned. "I think we're early, man," he said.

"Awesome," Otto replied. "I want to get in a test run before Hightop Lane is lousy with lugers."

"It's totally cool Mr. B was able to get this street closed all day for us!" Sam said.

"Gosh, it's awfully steep," Sam said with a gulp. "These luge boards don't come with brakes!"

"All the more reason to practice on a *real* street," Otto said. "Twister, make sure you shoot all my moves. I'll want to review the tape later."

Twister gave Otto a cheery thumbs-up. "No fear, man. My camera's battery is fully charged."

Twister began to walk backward down Hightop Lane, videotaping his buddies as they got ready for the practice run.

"You know, maybe a sport played on the street wasn't my best idea," Sam said.

"When I count to three, you guys hit it!" Twister called. "One . . two . . ."

"... three o'clock. That's when this street stooge tournament starts, right?" Mr. Black asked. Mr. Black was the head of the public works department of Ocean Shores.

"Luge, Mr. Black, street luge," Reggie replied. "Yes, that's the correct time."

"Good!" Mr. Black said. "You kids can set up the cones for the course after the street-cleaning machine washes everything down."

Reggie gasped. "B-But the course has already been set up! My brother and his friends are out there now!"

"Then they're going to get wet," Mr. Black said. "The cleaning truck has already left!"

"They can take the water—I'm worried about the impact," Reggie gasped. "Dad! Forget breakfast! We've got to get to Hightop Lane, and fast!"

"Trouble keeping up, Sam?" Otto called. "I know you can go faster than that!"

"You blaze the trail, Otto," Sam said through clenched teeth. "I'll follow your lead!"

"Then hurry up and follow me, Squid," Otto said, " 'Cause we're not stopping till we're at the bottom!"

Twister heard a rumbling noise behind him. At first he didn't know where it was coming from—until he felt drops of water splashing on his skin.

The weather forecast didn't mention a storm, he thought to himself as he turned to peer at the sky.

What he saw wasn't storm clouds. The street-cleaning machine turned onto Hightop Lane and was on a collision course with Otto and Sam!

Twist waved his arms and yelled at his friends. "Dudes! Watch out! Obstacle dead ahead!"

Otto gaped at the sight of the massive street-cleaning machine. There was only one option, and he hoped Sam could hang.

"Get ready to catch some air, Sam," Otto cried. "We're going curb hopping!"

One minute Sam and Otto were speeding along, wheels on the asphalt. The next, they were grabbing sky, the luge boards making the jump over the curb, right into a trash can.

"Otto! Sam! Are you all right?" Ray asked as he and Reggie rushed over to them.

"Totally, Dad," Otto said. "But one false move and we would have been street pizza with a side of roadkill!"

"Are we there yet?" a dazed Sam asked.

At three o'clock the tournament began without a hitch. The street was clean of dirt and debris—and instead was covered with young street lugers!

"Looks like Ocean Shores has another annual tradition," Ray said. "What do you think about that, Sam?"

"I think I've got to stop surfing the Internet," Sam moaned.